First Game Jitters

A Lady Pioneers Basketball Story

Season One: Game One

By: David White

Thank you for purchasing First Game Jitters: A Lady Pioneers Basketball Story.

This is the **_second_** chapter in a season-long journey. The first chapter, more of a season prelude, is available for FREE on my Patreon and several other places online. Want to keep up with every game, every rivalry, every moment on and off the court?

Join me on Patreon for:

- New game-by-game short stories
- Bonus player profiles, character cards, and behind-the-scenes content
- In-universe game broadcasts and post-game recaps
- Exclusive cover art, mockups, and future series sneak peeks
- Community polls and story votes

Follow the Lady Pioneers all season long at:

- patreon.com/LadyPioneerHoops

Let's chase this season together.

Table of Contents

Dear Reader...5

Chapter 1...7

Chapter 2...18

Chapter 3...24

Chapter 4...38

Chapter 5...46

Chapter 6...57

Chapter 7...73

Chapter 8...84

Chapter 9...102

Dear Reader,

Welcome to Lady Pioneers Basketball.

This isn't just a basketball story. It's a season. A locker room. A sideline. A bus ride home after a bad loss. It's the nerves of Jersey Day and the adrenaline of a rivalry game. It's late-night texts between teammates, inside jokes, unspoken pecking orders, and the pressure no one outside the locker room ever quite understands.

You're not just reading about it — you're in it.

You'll notice the story is told two ways. Some moments unfold like a traditional story, from inside the gym, the locker room, or the players' heads. Others drop you right into the game broadcast, with student announcers calling the action in real time. I kept those sections visually different — different fonts, different style — because in a real high school season, nothing sounds quite like game night. And you deserve to experience both.

This book isn't polished. It's not supposed to be. It's sweat, pride, heartache, and grit. It's about the moments you remember forever, even if no one else saw them. About the games you wish you could have back, and the ones you'll never stop reliving in your head. If you've ever chased something bigger than yourself, you'll get it.

Thanks for stepping into this season with us. I hope you find a little of yourself in these girls.

See you at tip-off. — Coach White

Chapter 1

The gym had that weird energy again — loud on the outside, but quiet underneath. Balls bounced. Shoes squeaked. Coaches called things out that no one really responded to. Everyone was moving, but it didn't feel like anyone was all the way there.

Callie Hewitt wiped her hands on her shorts again. Fifth time, maybe sixth. She caught a pass from Mallory, nearly bobbled it, and fired a jumper that smacked the front of the rim, bounced into the air, and went right over the backboard.

"Next!" Coach Ford called, clearly annoyed but already focused on the next shooter.

Callie jogged to the back of the line, lips pressed tight.

Across the court, Makenzie Voss was in full chaos mode, laughing as she yanked down a rebound with way too much enthusiasm. She nearly elbowed Rowan in the face.

"Sorry!" she called, a little too loud. A couple of the girls laughed.

Harper Connolly and Delaney Brooks were leaning against the wall near the water coolers, whispering and trying not to laugh.

"Kat, are you tying those or trying to cut off circulation?" Harper asked with a grin.

Katlynn didn't look up. "They were loose," she said, pulling her laces tight for the third time in two minutes.

"Just making sure," Delaney chimed in. "Would hate for you to trip in front of Tucker tomorrow and ruin your whole love story."

"He's not coming," Katlynn said quickly, voice flat.

Delaney raised her eyebrows. "Aww. You guys are so cute when you're toxic."

Harper smirked behind her water bottle but didn't say anything.

Katlynn stood up without responding, grabbed a ball off the rack, and bounced it once — hard.

Mallory caught the whole exchange from the free throw line. Her stomach tightened slightly. Something was off with Kat lately — not just today — but she pushed the thought aside.

Focus.

Practice wound down in a haze of sweat and nerves. The drills hadn't changed, but everything felt heavier. Tighter. The Lady Pioneers were less than 24 hours away from their first real game, and it showed.

Callie pulled her headband off and wiped her face with her jersey. Her last jumper barely grazed the front of the rim, and she hadn't made a shot since they shot free throws about midway through practice.

"Alright, circle up," Coach Ford called out, one sharp clap for emphasis.

The girls jogged in. Some slow. Some stiff. Makenzie still had a little bounce in her step. Mallory looked steady as ever. Callie tried to keep her breathing even.

Coach Ford didn't raise her voice. She didn't need to.

"Tomorrow's game day. If you're not nervous, you're not paying attention. That's normal. What matters is what you do with it."

A couple heads nodded. Delaney popped her gum and got a look from Eliza.

"You've put in the work," Coach Ford went on. "Now it's about trust. Trust the reps, trust the team, trust yourself, and trust the gameplan."

She paused, eyes sweeping the group.

"Before we break—captain. You've voted. I've got the results."

The gym went quiet.

"Mallory. You've done everything we've asked. You've helped the freshmen get comfortable. You motivate your teammates and help direct the team. For what it's worth, I think your teammates made the right choice. Congratulations."

Mallory blinked — just for a second — then gave a quick, confident nod.

No one said a word. A couple of nods. The silence was enough.

Coach Harper stepped forward then, glancing around the circle.

"Bus leaves at 11:15 sharp tomorrow morning," he said. "Do *not* be late. JV tips at 1, but it's only two quarters — they don't have enough players for a full game. Varsity will start right after. Probably around 2."

Several players murmured quietly, doing the math in their heads.

"We're wearing green," Coach Ford added. "Bring your warm-ups, be game-ready when you step off the bus."

Makenzie raised a hand halfway. "Snacks?"

Coach Harper shook her head. "Whatever you pack. It's a short ride, and we're not stopping. Eat a small lunch before you get on the bus. Don't show up with just a granola bar and expect sympathy."

"Dang," Delaney muttered.

Ford ignored her. "Get some rest. Eat like athletes. No staying up late watching junk. You've worked too hard to show up sluggish."

A few heads dipped.

"Mallory — meet me in my office before you leave," Ford added. "The rest of you, stretch, hydrate, and get out of here."

Mallory clapped once. "Pioneers on three!"

The girls joined in, hands stacked.

"1... 2... 3 — Pioneers!"

The clap echoed as they broke the huddle, grabbing water bottles, shuffling toward the locker room. Game mode was setting in.

Callie slung her bag over her shoulder and moved slowly toward the baseline. Her legs felt heavier than they should've. Her head even more so.

Mallory caught up to her.

"You good?" she asked, not looking directly at her.

Callie nodded, but her voice was flat. "Yeah."

Mallory gave her a look — the kind that said *I don't believe you, but I'll let it slide for now.*

"Alright. Be early tomorrow. We'll get some shots up before we leave."

Then she was gone, cutting across the gym toward Coach Ford's office.

Callie stood there for another second. The green jersey was folded in her bag. Her heart thudded in her ears.

* * * * *

THE NERVES WEREN'T COMING TOMORROW. THEY WERE ALREADY HERE,
TUCKED INSIDE EVERY JERSEY BAG AND HALF-FINISHED FREE THROW.

* * * * *

Chapter 2

The house was too quiet.

Callie sat on the edge of her bed, elbows on her knees, staring at the green jersey draped over the back of her desk chair. The soft glow from her lamp made the fabric look even brighter — almost like it didn't belong in the same room with her.

#35.
Her number.
Her chance. Maybe.

She ran her fingers along the hem of the shorts folded neatly underneath it. She'd laid everything out earlier, thinking it would help her feel prepared. All it did was make her stomach hurt.

A buzz from her phone broke the silence. Group text — *Pioneers* 🏀 *Squad.*

Delaney:

> "Tmrw = showtime 🔥 🔥 🔥 "

Harper:

> "Rowan better not forget her jersey
> again lol"

Rowan:

> "one time 💀 "

Mallory:

> "If you wanna shoot before we leave
> coach will be there at 1030 I will to"

Callie stared at the screen but didn't reply. She wasn't in the mood for emojis and inside jokes.

A knock sounded at her door — not loud, but firm.

She sat up straighter automatically. "Yeah?"

Her dad stepped in without waiting. Arms crossed. Eyes scanning the jersey across the room.

"You ready?"

She nodded, not trusting her voice.

He stayed in the doorway. "Coach starting you?"

Callie shrugged, "Didn't say," she whispered, to prevent her voice from cracking.

He raised an eyebrow like he didn't believe her. "Well, you better be ready either way."

Callie nodded again.

"Don't play timid," he demanded. "You get your shot, you take it. Don't be out there trying to be nice. You've got fifteen points in you — minimum."

Her chest tightened.

"Scouts watch the first game," he went on, still standing. "Varsity means something now. You don't want to spend your season riding the bench because you played soft tomorrow."

She didn't respond. She couldn't.

He looked at her one more time — like he expected her to promise something — then turned and walked out. The door clicked shut behind him.

Callie sat there for a long moment. Still. Frozen.

Eventually, she stood and walked over to the chair. Picked up the jersey and held it to her chest.

It felt light. Way too light for something carrying this much weight.

She shut her eyes.

"Please let me be good enough," she whispered.

She didn't remember lying down, but at some point she was under the covers, curled on her side, the jersey folded against her ribs. Her phone buzzed again, but she didn't look.

Tomorrow wasn't coming. It was already here.

* * * * *

SOME PLAYERS SLEEP LIKE IT'S ANY OTHER NIGHT.

OTHERS CURL AROUND A JERSEY LIKE IT'S ARMOR.

* * * * *

Chapter 3

The bus hissed as it pulled into the gravel lot behind the gym, just past noon. A few players stirred from naps, earbuds popped out, jackets unzipped. They sat in front of a squat brick building that barely looked like a high school. No sign out front, just a gym tucked behind chain-link fences and a few half-dead trees. It felt like the kind of place you might accidentally win or accidentally break down in.

The ride over had been quiet, that usual mix of nerves and focus. A few girls whispered about nothing in particular — the science test, someone's brother getting kicked out of class —

while others plugged into their headphones and stared out the window. Makenzie sat beside Callie, nervously bouncing one knee as Callie flipped through a printout of the opposing team's MaxPreps roster.

"You already have it memorized," Makenzie pointed out.

Callie shrugged. "I like to be sure."

When they arrived, the gym was still mostly empty — a couple of early-arriving parents in the stands and a student worker setting up the scorer's table.

"Fifteen minutes," Coach Ford called out. "Let's get some shots up."

Balls flew. Energy snapped into place. JV and varsity players scattered into their own rhythms.

Sienna called for rebounds. Noelle shot corner threes like she was trying to impress someone. Harper and Rowan locked into a two-player drill like they'd done it together a thousand times. The JV-only girls — Reagan, Ivy, Alyssa, Madeline, and Jenna — ran basic shooting lines, all tight shoulders and half-glances toward the bleachers.

Makenzie clutched her ball a second longer than most. Her fingers were stiff, like they'd forgotten how to grip.

Callie noticed. "You good?"

Makenzie gave her a tight smile. "First game since sixth grade. So, no."

"Ah. Cool cool," Callie said. "Just a game. Just lights, refs, parents, bleachers, teammates, and your entire athletic identity on the line."

Makenzie gave her a shove. "You're the worst."

But she stepped into a shot. Front rim. Chased it down. Tried again. Miss. Again. Swish.

"Better," Callie said with a wry smile.

Nearby, Delaney missed a floater and muttered, "I swear these rims are bent."

"Or maybe," Eliza offered without looking up, "you just suck."

Delaney grinned. "Fair point."

As the girls found rhythm, Coach Ford stood with the athletic trainer near the sideline. They spoke low. Harper leaned in.

"No Katlynn?" she asked.

Ford shook her head. "Texted me this morning. Said she wasn't feeling well. Mom said stomach issues."

Delaney, passing by with a Gatorade, snorted. "Translation: Tucker drama."

Ford gave her a look.

"I'm just saying," Delaney said, shrugging. "He Snapped his ex last night. Probably broke her again."

"Delaney," Harper said, trying not to laugh.

"What? The girl needs a breakup playlist and a therapist."

Ford crossed Katlynn's name off her clipboard without comment.

The buzzer sounded. The red numbers on the scoreboard flipped to 20:00.

Makenzie, Callie, Tessa, Mallory, Delaney, and Eliza drifted toward the locker room hallway. A few hit the concession stand. Makenzie and Callie shared a bag of popcorn, though Makenzie mostly just held the bag while Callie ate.

"Still nervous?" Callie asked between mouthfuls.

Makenzie nodded. "I think my hands are sweating through my socks."

Delaney passed them, a giant pretzel in hand. "If you faint mid-layup, I'll catch you. For the drama."

"You sure Katlynn didn't just fake sick to avoid Tucker?" Callie added.

Delaney took a theatrical bite. "Stomach issues. Stomach flipped when he said 'u up?' to his ex."

Makenzie laughed, barely. "I wish I had that excuse."

"No worries," Delaney said. "You'll kill it. Or you'll pass out and become a meme. Either way, memorable."

The girls eventually trickled back to the court, just as the JV warmups began. They settled behind the bench — uniforms crisp, legs crossed.

Sienna jogged past, already flushed. "Calling it now: first bucket's mine."

Delaney leaned toward Makenzie. "Think Brynn will trip over the free-throw line again?"

"Let's hope not," Makenzie said. "I can't handle that much secondhand embarrassment."

Alyssa and Reagan started high knees at half court. Ivy bounced in place like she might sprint out of the gym. Madeline adjusted her ponytail. Again. Jenna looked like she might cry.

Makenzie stared at the court, popcorn forgotten.

And just like that, the ref stepped into the circle with the ball.

"Here we go," Callie whispered.

Makenzie inhaled.

And the season officially began.

The JV half was a blur.

The scoreboard ticked upward like it was on autopilot. The Pioneers racked up buckets in every way — fast breaks, bank shots, even a weird-looking three from Brynn that arced so high it nearly kissed the rafters.

Their opponents, the Brush Run Ridge Runners JV team, barely managed a few baskets. By the five-minute mark, it was clear this wasn't going to be close.

Coach Harper, who coached the JV team, subbed in waves, rotating girls every few minutes. The pace never dropped — Ivy swiped three steals in one shift, Noelle dropped a dime to Sienna, and even Jenna, not exactly known for finesse, buried a baseline jumper that sent the bench into chaos.

The varsity players, those not suited up for JV, sat behind the bench — half-watching, half-chatting.

"She actually made that?" Delaney blinked as Brynn's rainbow shot fell through. "Physics is fake."

"Ivy's got like four steals already," Callie said, shaking her head.

"She always plays like she just drank three Red Bulls and a Mountain Dew," Eliza muttered.

Makenzie mostly watched in silence, eyes flicking from the court to the scoreboard to the gym door. Her fingers fidgeted with the edge of her jersey.

And then, right on cue — drama.

The gym doors squeaked open, and Tucker strolled in like he'd been cast as "trouble" in a teen drama. Hoodie half-zipped, AirPods in, arm slung around a brunette in leggings and a crop top. She laughed too loud at something he whispered.

"Oh no," Delaney whispered.

Callie groaned. "Is he serious right now?"

The girl leaned in close, whispering something that made Tucker grin — but he wasn't looking at her. His eyes scanned the court, skipped over the game entirely, and landed on the bench.

He gave the girl a casual squeeze, said something that made her roll her eyes and pull out her phone, and then peeled away — like he hadn't just walked in draped all over her.

Tucker made a beeline toward the team bench, stopping just short where Callie sat stretching her calves.

"Hey," he said low, tugging one AirPod out. "Seen Katlynn?"

Callie raised an eyebrow. "Not here."

"I can see that," he muttered. "She okay?"

"I don't know," Callie replied. "She didn't come."

Tucker nodded, chewing the inside of his cheek. "Cool. Yeah. Thanks."

"She's sick," Delaney snapped. "Now go away."

He stayed planted for a beat too long, like he expected Katlynn to pop out from behind a water cooler or something.

Callie watched him for a second, then turned her attention back to the court.

Tucker finally drifted away, heading toward the bleachers — though not back to the girl he came in with. She was scrolling through her phone like she didn't even know he'd walked off.

Makenzie didn't say anything, but her jaw tightened.

"Boys are so exhausting," Delaney muttered, leaning back. "Someone hand me a pretzel before I file a restraining order on her behalf."

The scoreboard ticked past the four-minute mark.

Coach Ford caught Mallory's attention. "Varsity, locker room — go!"

The girls stood as one, filing out through the double doors. The gym buzzed with momentum and popcorn fumes.

And just like that, it was their turn.

* * * * *

YOU CAN REHEARSE THE MOTIONS. WARM UP THE
BODY.
BUT NOTHING PREPARES YOU FOR THE MOMENT
IT'S REAL.

* * * * *

Chapter 4

The locker room buzzed — not loud, not chaotic, but charged.

Shoes squeaked as players shifted on the benches, adjusting shorts, tucking in jerseys, and tugging laces tighter. The air smelled like fresh laundry, hand sanitizer, and nerves.

Makenzie sat near the end, elbows on her knees, hands clasped. She stared down at the tops of her Jordan's, wearing them in a game tonight for the first time. She'd spent an hour choosing them — something solid, supportive, nothing too flashy. But now, sitting here, they felt unfamiliar.

She took a slow breath. In. Out. In again.

"You good?" Eliza asked from across the row, tying her braid into a final tight knot.

Makenzie nodded without looking up. "Yeah. Just... focused."

Coach Ford stepped into the center of the room, whiteboard under one arm, clipboard in the other.

"Alright. First things first — tonight's starters."

Callie glanced up casually, trying to appear calm and confident while her heart tried to escape her chest.

"Makenzie, you're starting at post. Just do what you've been doing in practice and you'll be fine," Coach Ford reassured her.

Makenzie swallowed hard, gave a small nod.

"Callie, you're the other post."

Callie's eyebrows shot up. Her chest fluttered. *Start?* She tried not to look around, not to let her excitement show. Her hands fidgeted at the hem of her jersey.

"Mallory, you got point. Eliza and Tessa, you're the wings."

Delaney cracked her knuckles and smiled. "Bench mob ready."

Rowan didn't react right away. She sat back, arms folded over her knees, eyes steady. She'd started last season, and everyone knew it. But she just nodded, cool and unreadable.

Coach Ford flipped to a clean board and started writing names and numbers.

"Matchups."
14 – Addie Rice – Eliza
22 – Jordan Watts – Tessa
33 – Maya Briggs – Makenzie
11 – Kelsey Shaw – Callie
5 – Bri Thomas – Mallory

Makenzie scanned the name and number she'd been assigned. She didn't recognize it — some tall kid with a double-digit number. But now it wasn't abstract. Now it was real. *That girl. That matchup. That paint.*

She squared her shoulders.

Next to her, Callie was still trying to process the word starter. It thudded in her ears like a heartbeat. *Don't mess this up.*

Coach clapped the whiteboard closed.

"Look — we've had this game circled for a while. I don't need perfect. I need intensity. I need smart decisions. I need every single one of you to be ready the second your number's called. Trust your teammates. Trust the gameplan. And if something goes sideways, stay calm and adjust. That's what good teams do. If you're on the floor, you earn your next minute. If you're on the bench, you're preparing to make the next play better than the one before. Questions?"

Silence.

"Let's go be us, ladies. If you want to pray, do that before you leave the locker room. Bring it in."

Mallory looked at Coach Ford, cracked a quick smile, their hands piled up, "Win on 3!"

"Ahhhhh, 1... 2... 3 — WIN!"

Coach left the room, the door swinging shut behind her.

The team stood still for a beat. Then Mallory cleared her throat.

"Let's pray."

Heads bowed. A circle formed instinctively, arms stretched across shoulders, sneakers tapping softly as they stood.

Mallory spoke, steady and low. "Lord, thank you for the chance to play tonight. Help us play hard and play together. Keep both teams healthy. Let us honor You with how we compete. Amen."

A quiet chorus echoed: "Amen."

Then the huddle broke.

Makenzie and Callie fell in step behind the group as they headed toward the gym doors, their footsteps light but their hearts pounding.

Time to go.

* * * * *

THERE'S A DIFFERENCE BETWEEN STEPPING ON THE
FLOOR
AND STEPPING INTO THE MOMENT. THIS WAS BOTH.

* * * * *

Chapter 5

The tunnel was dim, barely lit by the cracks of gym light sneaking in from the edges of the curtain. Echoes of crowd chatter, squeaking shoes, and the occasional over-amped voice from the student section created a kind of pulse just beyond the shadows.

Callie stood near the front, her eyes locked forward, jaw tight. Her hand kept flexing—open, closed, open again. She was trying to look composed. Locked in. But her foot tapped slightly. Her breath hitched when she thought no one was watching.

Next to her, Makenzie gave a soft chuckle under her breath, not at anything in particular. Her palms were slick. She wiped them on her shorts for the third time in as many minutes. Then she glanced sideways.

That's when it happened.

A look.

Quick, silent.

Callie, tense and trying to wear a face she didn't believe. Makenzie, smiling—barely—because it was the only thing she knew how to do when her stomach was in knots.

They didn't say a word. They didn't need to.

Callie's eyes said: "I have to prove something tonight."

Makenzie's said: "I have no idea if I belong here."

The music kicked up. The lights shifted.

"Let's go!" Mallory called from somewhere behind them.

The curtain parted. Two lines. One broke right, the other left.

The green jerseys of the Lady Pioneers spilled onto the court, a wave of nerves disguised as movement. The team split, forming two layup lines. Coaches nodded. A few parents clapped. The gym wasn't full, but it felt like the whole world was watching.

Callie hit her mark and cut to the hoop. She didn't remember if the ball went in. Maybe it bounced off. Maybe it swished. It didn't matter.

Her body moved, but her brain stayed stuck on loop: Don't mess up. Don't mess up. Don't—

Makenzie missed the first pass thrown her way. Her fingers felt like rubber. She smiled, of course —she always smiled—but it was more out of panic than joy. Her second catch was cleaner, but her shot airballed. She tried to laugh it off, but her eyes flicked to the bench. Did Coach see?

Across the court, the referees waved the captains over.

Mallory jogged out confidently.

Callie paused mid-drill to watch.

"One day," she thought, "that'll be me."

Then the whistle blew. Back to layups. Thirty seconds passed. Then a voice—Coach Ford's—cut through the white noise.

"Bring it in!"

The girls hustled to the sideline, sneakers scuffing. A quick huddle formed. Coach Ford's voice was low but firm.

"Eyes up. Talk on D. Stick to the gameplan. You've prepared for this."

The girls nodded. Callie breathed in deep.

"Let's go," Mallory said.

They lined up for the national anthem.

Silence.

Callie's heart pounded so loud she swore the person next to her could hear it. Her eyes darted to the other team's huddle, then back to the floor.

"Wait. Who was I supposed to guard again?" Her chest tightened. "Was it number 11? Or 14? Did Coach switch me?"

Panic. Real, clawing panic.

Next to her, Makenzie blinked slowly, eyes half-glazed. The anthem played, but her thoughts wandered. *This is happening. You're really starting. They trust you. Even if you don't trust yourself.* She smiled again, just a twitch. The kind you make when you're on the edge of laughing or crying but don't know which way you're gonna fall.

Anthem over. Applause.

Shooting shirts off.

The starters headed toward the bench, while the others formed a narrow tunnel, arms extended. Harper took her place at the end, already bracing for the flurry of handshakes, bumps, and quick words.

The announcer's voice buzzed over the mic—not hyped, not energized, just standard protocol.

"Starting for the Lady Pioneers…"

Each name, each number, read in order.

No crowd pop. No spotlight. Just shoes squeaking and the occasional claps from traveling parents in the corner.

One by one, the girls emerged from the tunnel, met Harper for a handshake—each one slightly different. Quick. Sharp. Ritualistic. Mallory. Boom. Eliza. Boom. Tessa. Boom. Makenzie. Boom. Callie. Boom.

As the final Lady Pioneer jogged out, the team hustled toward the free throw line.

Mallory was already in the middle, voice clear and quick.

"Hey. Eyes up. No one here expects us to come in and take this. So let's take it. Right now. For each other. Play hard. Trust the work."

Hands in.

"1... 2... 3 — Pioneers!"

As they broke, the lights dimmed.

Music kicked in. Spotlights swept across the floor. A mirrored disco ball scattered tiny constellations onto the back wall. The announcer's voice climbed, loud and proud, rattling the old bleachers.

"And NOW... YOUR LADY RIDGE RUNNERS..."

The home crowd erupted.

But the Lady Pioneers barely looked. Their focus was set.

Makenzie stepped to the center circle.

Callie stood a few steps behind, still buzzing, still unsure who she was guarding, still faking calm.

The ref tossed the ball in the air.

Makenzie's knees bent, arms up.

Okay, she thought, *just jump. Just make contact. Just don't miss.*

The ball floated up.

Everything else went quiet.

* * * * *

TIP-OFF ISN'T THE START OF THE GAME.
IT'S THE START OF PROVING WHO YOU ARE — AND
WHO YOU'RE NOT.

* * * * *

Chapter 6

"*Welcome to Pioneer Nation Basketball, live from Brush Run High School! Mike and Macy here, and yes, folks — it's finally game day!*"

"*About time, Mike. Been counting down since the scrimmage. Let's see if the Pioneers brought their game faces — or just their matching warmups.*"

"*Makenzie wins the tip — flicks it to Tessa — she pushes ahead to Mallory — over to Callie on*" *the wing — pull-up three — splash! First bucket of the season!"*

"Callie Hewitt woke up dangerous. That release was smooth."

"On the defensive end, Mallory gives Callie a little shove and points across the floor. Oops. Musta been guarding the wrong person. Great leadership from Mallory. First game jitters in full effect. Brush Run coughs it up — Makenzie with the scoop and outlet — Mallory up the sideline — bounce to Tessa sprinting the floor — layup's good."

"Two possessions, two buckets. Coach Ford might not hate this."

"Brush Run bricks one — Makenzie with the board, gets fouled, but no call. Still gets it to Mallory. This time, they set it up. Ball reversal — Eliza open in the corner — lets it fly — and buries it! Pioneers up 7–0 just like that."

"Eliza's shot looked like she never stopped warming up."

"Coach Ford's making her first subs — here comes Delaney, Harper, and Rowan."

"Delaney's already chirping before she even checks in. Gotta love the consistency."

"Rowan's in for Voss, Harper for Tessa, and Delaney for Callie. Let's see if the energy drops. Doesn't look like it. Mallory with a drive — draws two — kick to Harper — three on the way — ohh just off. But Rowan fights for the board — resets it. Eliza fakes, drives baseline — dishes to Delaney — up with it — no good, but she gets her own miss and finishes."

"Scrappy bucket. That's very Delaney. Missed it just to pat her rebounding stats."

"Brush Run finally hits a couple — back-to-back threes. Crowd's awake now."

"Coach Ford's not rattled — Tessa and Makenzie check back in, Callie's coming in too — Mallory, Rowan, and Eliza to the bench."

"Makenzie's already back on the boards —
grabs one off a miss, goes up strong — and
one! She's flexing. Did she just flex?"

"Can't confirm, but it was either a flex or a
cramp."

"She steps to the line — crowd buzzing — and
knocks down the free throw. Three-point play
for Voss!"

"Pioneers up 12–6 now. Let's see if they close
the quarter strong."

"Callie's back in — gets a high screen from
Makenzie — two dribbles — pulls up from the
elbow — got it."

"That's five already. She's not hesitating, Mike."

"She's dialed in. No second-guessing. Just hoops. Brush Run finally gets one to fall — tough floater in traffic. Cuts it to 14–8. Pioneers with the ball — six seconds left in the quarter — Harper swings to Delaney — she attacks the lane — takes the bump — finishes anyway! Buzzer beater from Brooks as the horn sounds! She took the contact and still gave the ref the 'seriously?' face."

"That was a foul, Mike. But hey, two points and a dramatic glare? Classic Delaney."

"And that wraps the first — Pioneers up 16–8 on the road. Callie's got five, Delaney with four off the bench, Makenzie with three, Eliza and

Tessa each with a bucket — and Mallory's quietly stacking dimes."

"Strong start, Mike. Let's see if they can keep it rolling in quarter two."

"Welcome back to Brush Run High School, where the Lady Pioneers take a 16–8 lead into the second quarter."

"They looked sharp in the first, Mike. Real sharp. Let's see if they can keep it rolling."

"Brush Run starts with the ball, working it slowly around the perimeter. The tempo's different already. Skip pass goes to the left corner — pump fake — drives baseline — soft floater goes up… and drops in. First points of the quarter go to the Ridge Runners."

"And uh, Mike… something's weird with this defense. I don't know what I'm looking at."

"That's a 2–3 zone, Macy. They're packing it in now, daring the Pioneers to shoot over the top. And based on the way the girls are standing around, I'm not sure they expected it."

"Yeah, Callie just passed it to where no one even was. Straight into the bench."

"Turnover leads to a quick push — Ridge Runners skip it ahead to the same corner — catch and shoot three — and it's good. Just like that, it's a three-point game. The Pioneers *still look lost. Second straight possession, same confusion — Mallory starts the offense, looks middle, nobody is there. Tries to swing it — and it sails out of bounds. Ball back to the Ridge Runners. They don't hesitate — attacking immediately off the inbound, quick drive, draws the help, she kicks to the wing — another three on the way… and it's good again. We're all tied up at sixteen."*

"Coach Ford immediately calls for time. You could hear her clap from here, Mike. Looks like first game jitters are officially in the building."

"She's probably simplifying it. Get them a zone-buster look, calm the nerves, and bring in some spark. And here come the subs — Harper, Rowan, and Delaney."

"Oh boy. This is about to get feisty."

"Pioneers coming out of the timeout now —
Mallory up top, patient this time. Swings it to
Delaney on the short wing — Rowan cuts hard
through the middle — Delaney feeds her —
clean catch, clean layup. That's how you do it,
Macy. That's a textbook way to beat the zone."

"Oh wow, look at you, Coach Mike. Should I
start calling you Clipboard?"

"Only if you spell it right. Now here comes the
press — Harper slaps the floor, crowd gets into
it — and she pokes it loose! The ball bounces
free — Harper dives — she somehow flips it
over to Rowan — wide open under the basket

— lays it in! Back-to-back buckets for Rowan McClain."

"Now, that's how you swing momentum."

"But the Ridge Runners aren't slowing down. Quick inbound, they beat the press this time — Callie's trying to recover, but she's behind the play — layup goes up over her outstretched arm — and it falls. That's 20–18."

"Come on Callie! Pay attention!"

"Easy, Macy. She tried. Pioneers slow it down again — Tessa gets a great look inside — high off the glass — too strong. Delaney crashes in and grabs the miss Pump fake. She powers it *back up through contact. No whistle, but what a finish! 22–18 Pioneers."*

"Delaney's stronger than she looks, Mike!"

"Ridge Runners try to attack quickly, great help defense by Rowan. They're forced to pull it back out, reset their offense — oh no, they've been hitting threes all night — and here comes another. Clean release… and it's good. They're within one."

"They can really shoot!"

"Mallory walks it up, passes to Callie on the wing. Callie gets aggressive — drives hard, draws the bump — gets to the line."

"She needed that, Mike. She's trying to will herself back into this game."

"Callie steps up to the line, receives the pass from the ref. The gym's gotten louder somehow. She spins the ball, takes a deep breath, eyes the rim, and lets it fly — back iron. No good."

"You can see it, Mike. She's not even mad. She's thinking. She's remembering every time she missed those last year. It's all bubbling up again."

"She'll get this one, though. Catches the ball — dribble, breath, release — short. Front rim. Ridge Runners snatch the rebound and go — they don't even hesitate — push it up the right sideline, now to the middle — a little hesitation move — pulls up for the floater in the paint — Callie tries to recover — late — and she's fouled on the shot."

"I can't believe that went in, Mike. Tie game with four seconds left in the half! This gym just flipped."

"The Ridge Runners have taken their first lead of the game — 23 to 22. She steps to the line now. Ball in hand. One bounce. Everyone's on their feet. Shot is up… and good. The Ridge Runners now lead 24 to 22. The Pioneers will try to respond here — inbound to Mallory — she pushes up the sideline — skips it ahead to Harper — just out of reach — she's got to save it — can't get to it! Out of bounds as the buzzer *sounds. And just like that, the first half is over. The Ridge Runners stormed all the way back after trailing by eight after one to take a one-point lead into halftime."*

"That's a tough walk to the locker room, Mike. You can feel it. Shoulders low. Heads down. That first-quarter confidence is nowhere to be found."

"Halftime score from Brush Run: Ridge Runners 24, Lady Pioneers 22. We'll be back after the half for more action. Don't go anywhere."

* * * * *

HALFTIME DOESN'T LIE. IT JUST SHOWS YOU
WHAT THE SCOREBOARD COULDN'T.

* * * * *

Chapter 7

The buzzer sounded, and the Lady Pioneers trudged off the court, sneakers squeaking across the polished floor. No one said much. A few half-hearted high-fives. A couple of shrugs. Mallory caught Callie's eye and gave her a quick nod — *stay with it* — but Callie just looked down at her shoes.

The locker room door swung open with a metallic clank, and the girls filed in slowly. No music. No chatter. Just the heavy weight of a lead lost.

They slumped onto benches, chests heaving, jerseys soaked through. No coaches yet. Just them.

For a long moment, it was silent — the occasional click of a water bottle cap, the sound of someone unlacing their shoes, the thump of a knee brace hitting the floor.

Then Delaney broke the quiet.

"Well... that sucked," she muttered.

A few nervous laughs escaped the circle. Harper nudged her shoulder into Delaney's. "We're fine. Just gotta make shots."

"No, we gotta stop turning it over every two seconds," Eliza grumbled, peeling off her headband and flinging it across the floor.

"The zone's messing us up," Mallory said, voice low and even. "We're rushing. Forcing everything."

Callie didn't say anything. She just sat with her elbows on her knees, bouncing one leg like it was trying to outrun the half.

Makenzie wiped her face with her jersey. "I forgot all the plays," she said, earning a few tired chuckles and a lopsided grin from Tessa.

Out in the hallway, the coaches huddled.

Coach Ford spoke first. "Shot selection is killing us."

Coach Harper nodded. "And turnovers. I swear every point they've got came after a bad pass."

"We're not adjusting to the zone," Ford added, tapping her finger against the whiteboard. "We need a flash to the high post. Short corner's been wide open."

"They're running everything through that point guard — Number 14. Addie Rice," Harper said. "Quick first step, and she's got vision. Either scoring or finding shooters."

Ford nodded sharply. "We take her away, we take the game back."

Back at the locker room door, Coach Ford knocked once and called out, "Everyone good?"

A few voices answered — "Yeah," "We're good," "You can come in."

She opened the door and stepped inside, Coach Harper right behind her.

Coach Ford didn't yell.

She didn't need to.

"Listen up," she said, voice low but razor-sharp. "You're not tired. You're not outmatched. You're just playing stupid."

No one blinked. Not even Delaney.

"You let them switch defenses on you, and you panicked. You let one girl beat you off the dribble — over and over. You're not thinking. You're reacting."

She paced slowly in front of them, her eyes scanning the room like she was memorizing every face.

"We're not losing because they're better. We're losing because we're handing them the ball on a silver platter."

She stopped dead center. Looked them all in the eye.

"So here's what we're going to do."

She turned to the old green chalkboard — scarred from seasons of dust and tape and frustration — and began writing with short, sharp strokes of yellow chalk.

OFFENSE VS ZONE – 1–2–2 SET

- Mallory or Tessa flashes high post
- Look to short corners
- PATIENCE! Not everything needs to be a three

DEFENSE

- Full-court *man* press after made baskets
- RUN & JUMP when we trap
- Get the ball out of Rice's hands

She turned back to the group.

"After every made basket, we're in full-court man. Run-and-jump. I want that ball out of Rice's hands before she crosses half court. Trap her. Force her to give it up early."

Then she glanced at Coach Harper. "Got anything?"

He nodded. "Yeah — when we trap, everybody rotates. If they swing it, we cover down and recover up. No freelancing. And we *finish* the possession. Box out and get the rebound."

Ford gave a single nod, then looked at the whole room again.

"And finally — play. your. game. Quit second-guessing every pass. Quit rushing every shot. You know how to play. Trust yourself."

She let it hang. Just long enough.

"You're lucky you only gave up 24. Should've been 40 the way you played."

A few heads dipped lower.

Then — the shift. A slight softening.

"But it's 24–22. One possession. Nothing we can't fix."

Ford cracked the faintest smile. The kind that didn't reach her eyes but still meant something.

"Now let's go take our game back."

A single clap echoed through the room as the girls stood in unison. Jerseys tugged down. Headbands resecured. Shoulders set. They formed a circle, hands in.

"Pioneers on three," Mallory said.

"1... 2... 3 — PIONEERS!"

They broke the huddle and headed out, sneakers squeaking again, this time with a little more purpose.

Near the tunnel, Callie's dad was waiting.

He didn't yell. Didn't say much.

Just stepped in close and muttered, "Be more aggressive."

Callie barely met his eyes. Just gave a quick nod and jogged to catch up with the others.

Whatever she was carrying, it was coming with her into the second half.

* * * * *

SOME PLAYERS SHAKE OFF THE FIRST HALF.
OTHERS CARRY IT LIKE A SECOND UNIFORM.

* * * * *

Chapter 8

"*Welcome back to Pioneer Nation basketball! Mike and Macy here from Brush Run, where the Lady Pioneers trail by two — 24-22 — as we get set for the second half.*"

"*Bit of a mess in the second quarter, Mike, but they're still right there. This thing's wide open.*"

"*Appalachian Trail starts with the ball on the sideline. Mallory to inbound, and we're back underway. Mallory hits Eliza on the wing, then cuts through the lane — pops up at the high*" *post — gets it right back — rips baseline — kicks to the corner — Voss catches, rises, and buries it!"*

"She didn't even blink. Just caught and fired like she's been waiting all day."

"24 all, and the Pioneers jump into full-court man. Callie picks up ball-side, Mallory and Voss closing space — pass tipped — Eliza dives! Keeps it alive but just rolls out of bounds. Still Ridge Runner ball."

"Eliza's already got more floor burns than points, Mike."

"Brush Run resets — swing to the top — drive and kick — open corner three — off the back

iron. Callie snatches the rebound. That's a strong board. And here come the Pioneers — Mallory slowing it down — swings left to Eliza — skip to Voss — open again — lets it fly — good again!"

"Do not let that girl stay in the corner, Mike. That's a warning shot."

"Brush Run brings it up — good movement — quick post feed — turn and finish. Nice answer. 26 all. Mallory brings it across — motion offense — reversal to Eliza — into Voss — kicks back to Mallory — entry to Tessa — spin move — left hand off the glass!"

"Tessa Aldridge doing what she does best."

"Brush Run wastes no time — Rice pushes — dishes last second — easy two. 28–28, Pioneers trying desperately to hold onto a lead. Back on offense now — Mallory flips it to Eliza — skip pass to Callie on the wing — one hard dribble — pull-up jumper… off the mark. And she's watching it — not crashing — and now her eyes are up in the stands."

"Yeah, she's looking right at her dad, Mike. That's not where her focus needs to be."

"And here come the Ridge Runners the other way — long pass up the sideline — nobody back — layup good. That's two points on a mental mistake. Brush Run back into the lead. Next possession — Mallory brings it up — Callie drifts to the corner — gets the pass — tries to *whip it inside to Tessa — tipped — out of bounds! Dead ball — and here comes the sub. Delaney Brooks checks in, and Callie jogs straight to the bench."*

"Coach Ford's waiting — one hand on her hip, the other on the clipboard. Calm words, but you know they hit."

"Pioneers ball again — Mallory up top — swings it to Voss — little pressure — she gives it up to Eliza — ball tipped! Eliza dives! Saves it with a slide! Gets it to Mallory — two steps, scoop — and it goes!"

"Strong take through traffic. Pioneers tie it back up."

"Brush Run calls timeout. And we've got a wave of subs coming in — here comes Sienna Rhodes, Harper Connolly, and Rowan McClain. That'll reset the floor — it's Mallory, Delaney, Harper, Rowan, and the new face — Sienna Rhodes making her Pioneer debut."

"She doesn't look nervous, Mike."

"Nope — and she played AAU with Mallory and Rowan over the summer. She knows these girls. Back from the timeout — Ridge Runners inbound — Pioneers stay full-court — trap in the corner — ball tipped by Mallory — loose — Delaney dives — tie-up!"

"Jump ball! Arrow to Appalachian Trail."

"Harper to inbound — gets it to Mallory — swings it to Rhodes — her first touch — quick trigger from the wing… drains it!"

"Okay then! Who is this kid? She fits like she's been here for years."

"Brush Run looking shaky now — try to throw over the trap — too tall — out of bounds. Pioneer ball. Here they come again — Mallory across midcourt — flips it to Rhodes — catch and fire — another one!"

"Back-to-back triples! Sienna Rhodes is on fire! Pioneers up 36–30!"

"Brush Run finally calms down — swing and attack — layup good. Mallory sets it up —

Harper on the wing — down to Rowan in the short corner — skip to Delaney — back to Rhodes — one dribble — floater — drops in!"

"She's got eight and looks like she's been in this rotation for months. 38–32."

"Brush Run tries to respond — long shot — off — Rowan taps it — Delaney crashes — Harper dives and ties it up! Another jump ball!"

"Arrow stays with Brush Run — but that's three different Pioneers on the floor."

"Final minute — Mallory calls for a clearout — swings to Delaney — 15-footer — money. Brush Run hurries — wild three — off the mark — Rowan grabs the rebound — hands it off to

Harper — and that's the quarter! Pioneers storm back — they lead 40–32 heading to the fourth!"

"Mike, that was hustle, depth, and a little rookie magic."

"Everything Coach Ford drew up at halftime is working — and Rhodes just added a whole new wrinkle."

"Fourth quarter underway here at Brush Run, and Coach Ford rolls out the starters... almost. It's Mallory, Tessa, Eliza, Makenzie, and, surprise . . . Sienna on the floor. Callie still on the bench."

"I mean… would you take out the hot hand, Mike? Sienna's on fire."

"Rhodes picks up right where she left off — catch and shoot from the wing… and drains it! That's 11 for her."

"She's cooler than a snow cone, Mike. That shot barely touched the net."

"Brush Run looks to answer — drive inside — denied by Voss! Eliza snags the loose ball and hands it off to Mallory. Mallory surveys the floor — bounce pass to Tessa running the sideline… she pulls up from deep — three on the way… money!"

"Now that is confidence, Mike. You sure she's not a guard? That gives Tessa 7 points on the night."

"Next Brush Run trip — wild pass — stolen by Eliza! Pioneers in transition — Mallory swings it to Sienna — she looks off the defender — steps in — midrange jumper — good! 13 for Rhodes. Brush Run comes back the other way — quick shot — bounces long — Tessa tracks it down — they're running again. Back to work — Mallory finds Voss inside — skips to Tessa again — from the wing this time — three ball... yes!"

"Tessa Aldridge heating up late. She's up to 10. Pioneers stretch the lead — it's 51–32 now. Brush Run calls timeout.

"Coach Ford meets the team with a grin. That's an 11-nothing run to open the quarter."

"Back from the timeout — Brush Run gets a bucket on a nice cut inside."

"Pioneers respond — Sienna with a skip pass to Tessa — she attacks the closeout, steps into a long two... got it! That's 12 for Aldridge."

"Brush Run goes quick again — another floater falls. 53–34."

"Mallory up top — she finds Sienna drifting into the corner — catch, shoot — bottom! That's 16 for Rhodes."

"Next Ridge Runner trip — off the mark — Eliza boards it strong."

"Mallory swings it early to Tessa — rhythm three from the left wing — drills it! That's 15 for her."

"Now it's 59–34 with just under 3 to play."

"Brush Run gets a desperation heave to fall — makes it 59–37."

"Coach Ford signals. Wholesale subs checking in. Callie, Harper, Rowan, Noelle, and Brynn take the floor."

"Harper pressures the ball near midcourt — jumps the passing lane — clean steal! Pioneers reset in the halfcourt."

"Callie swings it to Harper on the wing — she tries to fire it to the top of the key — but it's picked clean by Brush Run — coast-to-coast layup."

"That pass was so bad it came with a gift receipt."

"Next possession — Harper open for three — airball."

"Yikes. That one had altitude sickness."

"Brush Run pushes it again — fast break — but Rowan steps in to draw a charge!"

"Big moment there — might slow things down."

"Coach Ford calls timeout. She gathers the group. A couple quick points, drawing something up. Clipboard's out."

"Back on the floor — play in motion — ball swings through Callie and Rowan — Harper rotates to the top — feet set — nails it! Redemption three."

"Now she's one for three, Mike. Batting .333."

"Final minute now. Callie trying to get a bucket — spins in the lane — misses. Gets her own board — back up — no good. That's rebound number eleven."

"She's working, but nothing's falling."

"Next trip — foul on Brush Run — Callie to the line. First free throw… good. Second one… off the back rim."

"That's her only point since the first quarter, Mike, but she's done the dirty work tonight."

"This should be the final possession for the Pioneers — thirty seconds to go — Noelle has it — little hesitation — finds Brynn cutting backdoor — layup good! Her first varsity bucket!"

"Look at the bench, Mike. That's joy right there."

"And that'll do it. Final horn sounds, and it's all Lady Pioneers — they win it big on the road, 65–39."

"Rhodes leads all scorers with 16. Tessa right behind her with 15. Eight other players scored. Mallory with 12 assists. Callie pulled down 11 rebounds. Total team win."

"Go Pioneers, Mike. That's how you start a season."

* * * * *

A TEAM WIN ON THE COURT. A GREAT SECOND HALF
SEALED THE DEAL
FOR THE LADY PIONEERS. WAS WINNING ALL THAT
MATTERED?

* * * * *

Chapter 9

The locker room wasn't loud.

Not at first.

Coach Ford stepped in and waited for the last shoe to drop on the tile floor.

Then: "One and oh," she said simply, voice calm. "That's the goal. Win the next one. Then the next."

She looked around at tired faces and sweat-matted hair.

"Lot to clean up. But for now?" She cracked a smile. "Proud of you."

A wave of cheers broke out — not wild, but real. Girls high-fived, bumped shoulders, a couple even laughed. Delaney did a full spin before flopping onto the bench.

Mallory sat with her back against her locker, thumbing open her phone. One message:

"1-0. We did it."

She stared at it for a second, then hit send. Katlynn wouldn't see it right away. But she'd see it eventually.

The hallway lights buzzed, flickering slightly above the trophy case. Callie trailed a step behind her parents — her dad's voice already setting the tone for the ride home.

"You should've scored more," he said flatly, holding the car keys like a judgment. "You're a starter now. That means something."

Callie blinked. Bit the inside of her cheek. Her response never made it past her throat.

Beside him, her stepmom gently touched his arm. Didn't say a word — just a look. He exhaled. Not quite apologetic. Just... done talking.

They moved on. Callie didn't follow right away.

Behind her, the gym doors creaked open again — louder now that the crowd had cleared.

She turned slightly, just enough to catch the sound of laughter.

Up the hall, Makenzie was all teeth. Her dad had both hands on her shoulders, face lit up like they'd just won a state title.

"Seven points, kiddo! You looked strong in there!"

"And five boards!" her mom added, lifting a phone before Makenzie could duck the camera.

"I even got one of the free throws," Makenzie said, voice sheepish.

"Hey — that 'and-one' was legit," her dad grinned. "You looked like a real post out there."

Makenzie smiled, wide and proud, her backpack swinging as they turned toward the lot. Her high-tops squeaked softly on the tile — not from nerves this time, but from joy that couldn't sit still.

Callie watched them until they turned the corner. Her hand brushed the strap of her own bag.

She looked down at her shoes. One still untied. Eleven rebounds. A good screen here, a help-side rotation there. Nothing highlight-worthy.

No picture.

No dad with his hands on her shoulders.

Just a starter who didn't start the fourth.

She swallowed hard, pulled her hoodie tighter around her, and stepped into the chill outside.

* * * * *

NEXT UP: THE HOME OPENER.
AND NOT EVERYONE WILL FEEL AT HOME.

* * * * *

Thank you for reading First Game Jitters: A Lady Pioneers Basketball Story.

This is the second chapter in a season-long journey. Want to keep up with every game, every rivalry, every moment on and off the court?

Join me on Patreon for:

- New game-by-game short stories

- Bonus player profiles, character cards, and behind-the-scenes content

- In-universe game broadcasts and post-game recaps

- Exclusive cover art, mockups, and future series sneak peeks

- Community polls and story votes

Follow the Lady Pioneers all season long at:

- patreon.com/LadyPioneerHoops

Let's chase this season together.

#LadyPioneers #HighSchoolHoops #BasketballFiction